DADDY'S MINI-ME

By Arnold Henry

Illustrated by Ted M. Sandiford

Piton Books

The Inspiration

After the birth of my son, I decided to take a year off work so that I could capture every moment of his life. Daddy's Mini-Me was created based on these proud and special moments that I was able to witness during his early developmental stages.

Daddy's Mini-Me by Arnold Henry
Illustrated by Ted M. Sandiford
Edited by Tracy Blaine & Melinda R. Cordell

The Cataloguing-in-Publication Data is on file at Library and Archives Canada

ISBN: 978-0-9940272-5-2 (Paperback)
ISBN: 978-0-9940272-6-9 (Hardcover)

www.arnoldhenry.com
www.daddysminime.com

For all the proud fathers who continue
to be present in their children's lives.

Hello fathers,
by signing this agreement below, you have made a
promise to always be a role model for your child or children.

I, _____,

promise to be the best father in the world to my

beautiful and amazing child/children,

_____.

Print Name: _____

Signature: _____

Daddy and Baby meet
for the first time.
"Wow," says Daddy.
"My Baby looks like a mini-me."

As time goes by,
Baby does what Baby sees.
Daddy is looking
as proud as can be.
My Baby acts just like me.

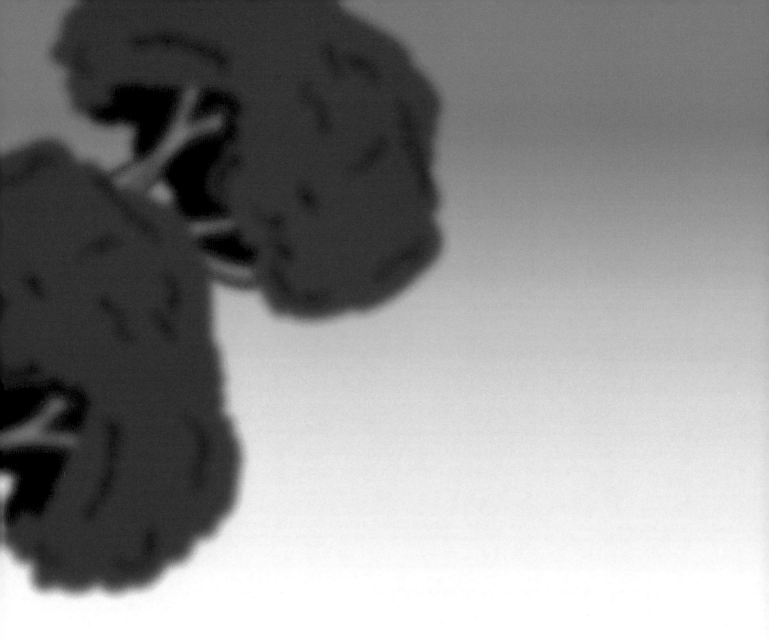

Daddy, Daddy, look at me!
I can smile when you smile at me.

I am looking.

I can see.

You can smile just like me.

Go...Go...Go my mini-me.

Daddy, Daddy, look at me!
I can roll on my back and tummy.

I am looking.

I can see.

You can roll just like me.

Go...Go...Go my mini-me.

Daddy, Daddy, look at me!
I can crawl on my hands and knees.

I am looking.
I can see.
You can crawl just like me.
Go...Go...Go my mini-me.

Daddy, Daddy, look at me!
I can stand on my feet like a tree.

I am looking.

I can see.

You can stand just like me.

Go...Go...Go my mini-me.

Daddy, Daddy, look at me!
I can clap then stomp my feet.

I am looking.

I can see.

You can clap then stomp like me.

Go...Go...Go my mini-me.

Daddy, Daddy, look at me!
I can hug and kiss Mommy.

I am looking.

I can see.

You can hug and kiss like me.

Go...Go...Go my mini-me.

Daddy, Daddy, look at me!
I can wave and say bye-bye.

I am looking.
I can see.
You can do it just like me.
Go...Go...Go my mini-me.

Daddy, Daddy, look at me!
I can brush my two front teeth.

I am looking.
I can see.
You can brush them just like me.
Go...Go...Go my mini-me.

Daddy, Daddy, look at me!
I can use my own potty.

I am looking.

I can see.

You can use it just like me.

Go...Go...Go my mini-me.

Daddy, Daddy, look at me!
I can say my ABC's.

I am looking.
I can see.
You can say them just like me.
Go...Go...Go my mini-me.

Daddy, Daddy, look at me!
I can count up to twenty.

I am looking.

I can see.

You can count them just like me.

Go...Go...Go my mini-me.

Daddy keeps looking as proud as can be.

My Baby will forever look up to me.

My Mini-Me.

Made in the USA
Columbia, SC
08 June 2020